HarperCollins®, ⬛*, and HarperKidsEntertainment™
are trademarks of HarperCollins Publishers.

Open Season: Home Is Where the Heart Is
™ & © 2006 Sony Pictures Animation, Inc. All rights reserved.
Printed in the United States of America.
No part of this book may be used or reproduced in any manner whatsoever without
written permission except in the case of brief quotations embodied in critical articles and reviews.
For information address HarperCollins Children's Books, a division of HarperCollins Publishers,
1350 Avenue of the Americas, New York, NY 10019.
www.harpercollinschildrens.com
Book design by John Sazaklis
Library of Congress catalog card number: 2006926473
ISBN-10: 0-06-084603-8 — ISBN-13: 978-0-06-084603-9

First Edition

OPEN SEASON™

Home Is Where the Heart Is

Written by
Jennifer Frantz

HarperKidsEntertainment
An Imprint of HarperCollinsPublishers

Ever since he was a grizzly cub, Boog had lived at Beth's house.
Beth cared for Boog as if he were her own child.

Boog grew bigger . . . and bigger . . . and bigger!
But he was still Beth's baby.

Boog and Beth loved to spend time together. And Boog could always make Beth smile. Deep down Beth knew that Boog belonged in the wild, but she couldn't imagine ever saying good-bye to him.

One day, while Beth was in Sheriff Gordy's office,
Boog saw something strange.
A scrawny one-horned mule deer named Elliot
was tied to the truck of the meanest hunter in town.

"Untie me!" Elliot pleaded to Boog.
"I don't want to be mounted on a wall!"
Boog thought about it for a while.
Then, with a swipe of his paw,
he set Elliot free.

Later that night, Boog had a surprise visitor.
It was Elliot, the mule deer he had rescued in town!

Elliot was lonely. He wanted Boog to be his friend and wanted him to come out and play. Boog never went outside without Beth, but he didn't want Elliot to think he was a mama's bear.

Boog and Elliot wandered around town searching for a midnight snack.
Soon they spotted the PuniMart—stocked with lots of tempting treats!

Boog and Elliot made a huge mess.
Sheriff Gordy showed up at the PuniMart.
Elliot managed to escape,
but Boog was caught red-*pawed*.

Sheriff Gordy drove Boog home to Beth.
Gordy nodded toward Boog. "It's time, Beth," he said.
Beth was upset, but she knew Gordy was right.
Boog was a wild animal. It was time for him to
go live out in the forest with other animals.

While Boog was asleep, Beth took him into the forest, high above the waterfalls. She hoped Boog would be safe from hunters up there.

When Boog woke up, his comfy house was gone and so was Beth.
All that was left was his teddy bear, Dinkelman.
He had to find a way to get back home!

Just when things couldn't get any worse, Boog found Elliot—
the troublemaker who'd caused this whole mess!
Elliot convinced Boog that he could help him find his way home.

But Boog and Elliot's journey was difficult.
They couldn't find their way home. They couldn't find a meal.
And they couldn't find any friends to help them.
All the other animals did was laugh at them—or *worse*—
throw acorns at them!

Tired from searching all day,
Boog and Elliot decided to sleep in the woods
and get a fresh start in the morning.

The next day, they suddenly heard a BLAST!
through the forest air.
"What was that?!" Boog asked.
"Hunters!" a beaver cried.
Open season had begun and all the animals
were in danger, including Boog and Elliot.

Boog and the other animals
soon realized they'd have
to work together to stop the
hunters. That very night
they made a plan to drive
the hunters out of the forest!

At dawn, they launched
their attack!
The frightened hunters
fled the forest. Boog
and the other animals rejoiced.
The forest was safe!

All of a sudden a helicopter
appeared in the sky. . . .
It was Beth! She was very
glad to find Boog safe.
"C'mon, let's go home!" she cried.
Boog was happy to see Beth,
too, but something inside
of him had changed.
It was time to say good-bye.

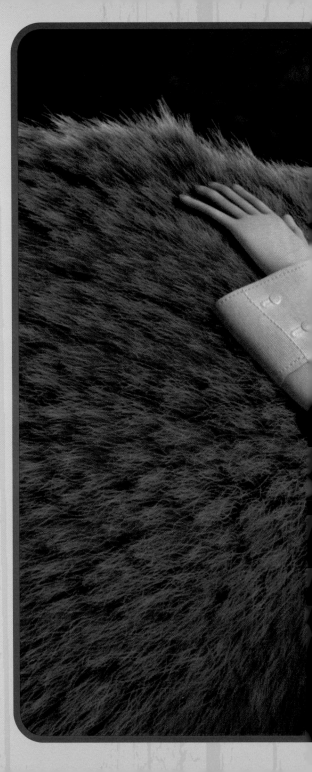

Boog took a deep breath of fresh forest air and smiled.
In his heart he knew he was finally home.